Too Many Clothes

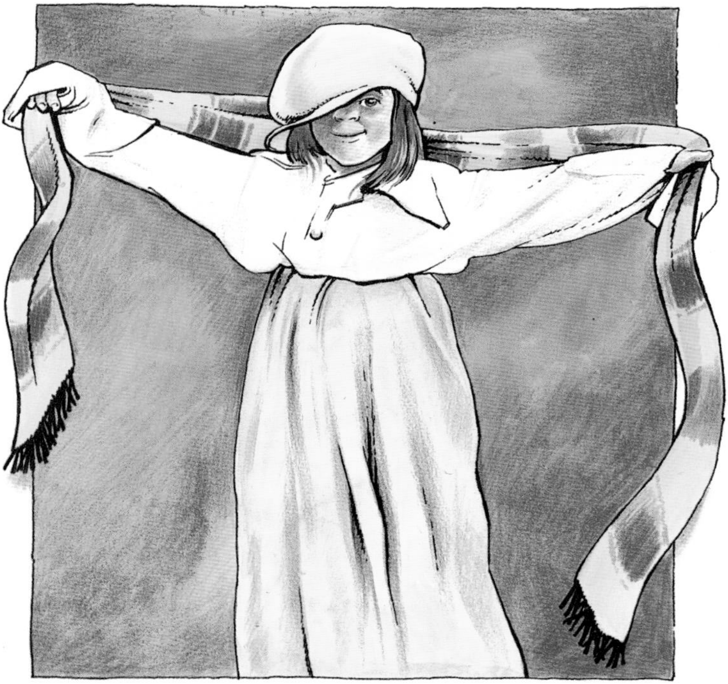

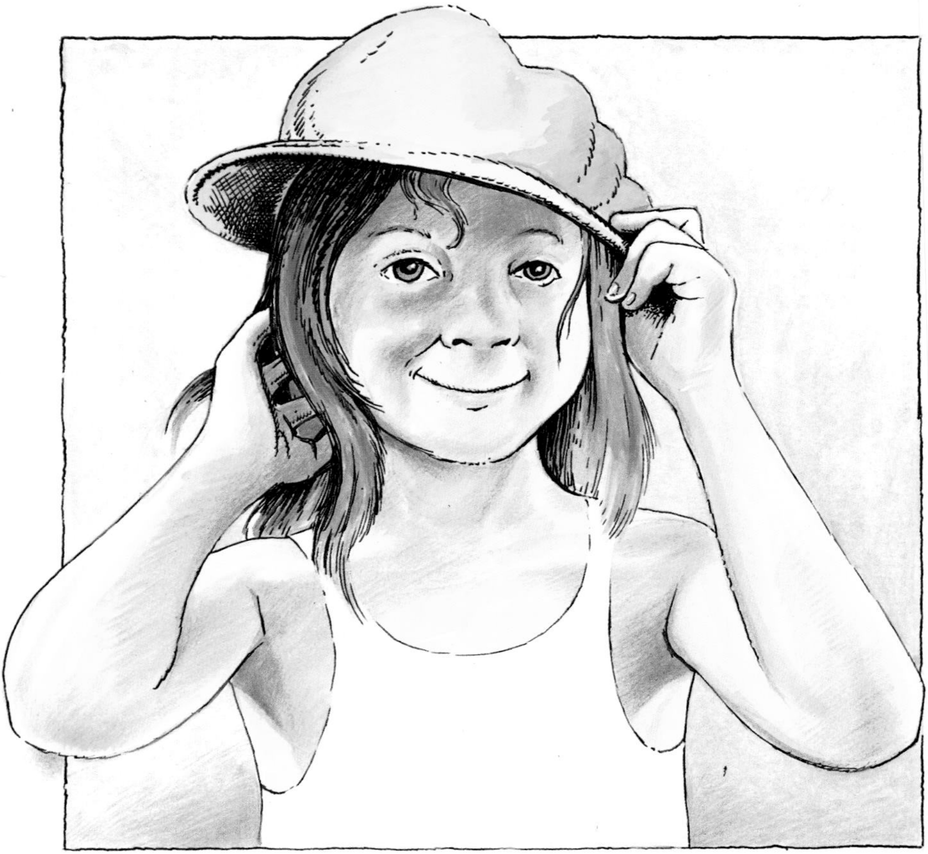

First, Dad's hat,

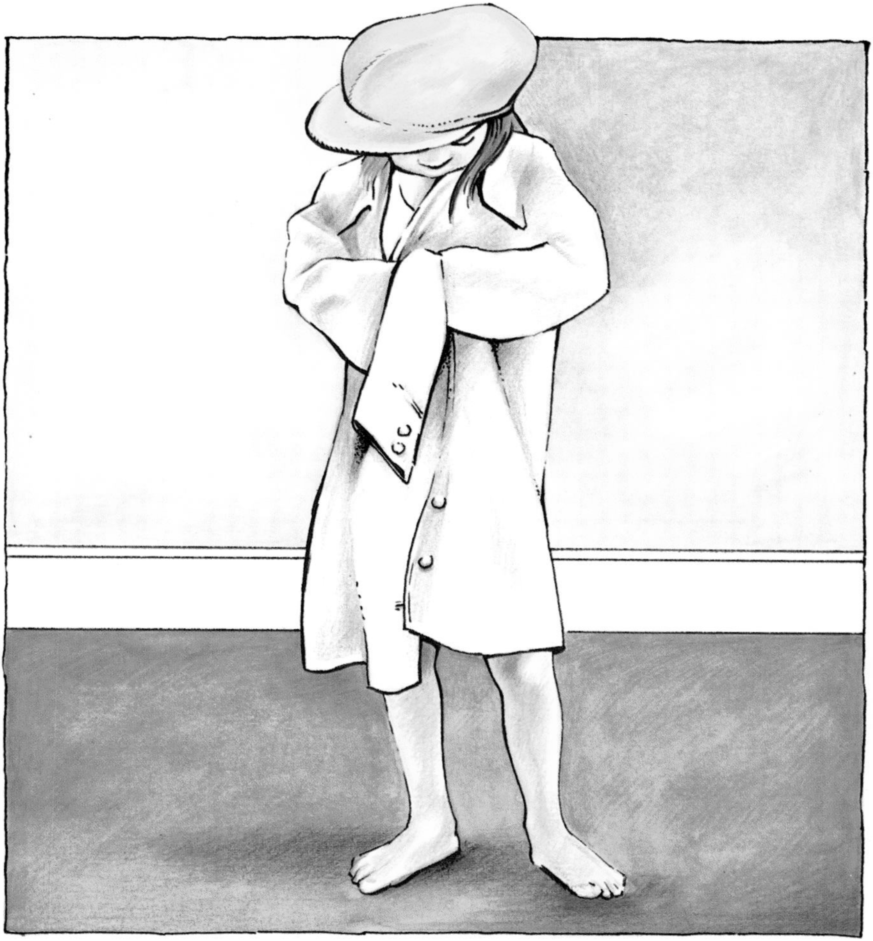

then Mom's shirt,

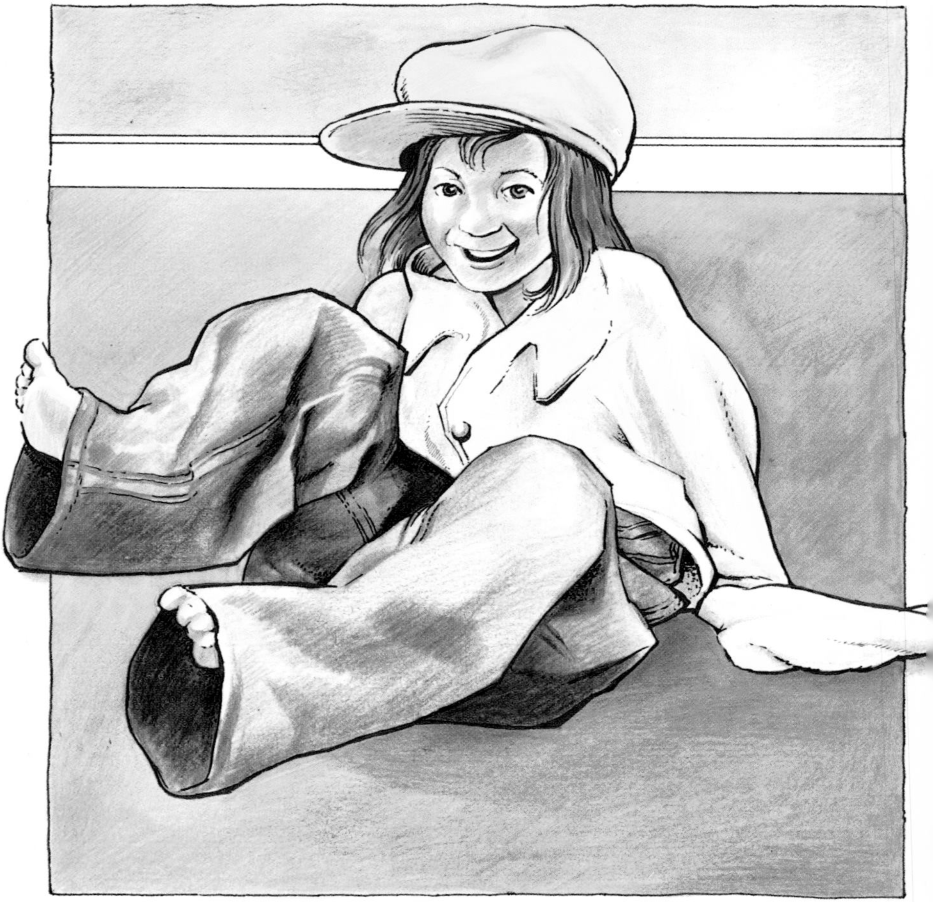

then Dad's jeans,

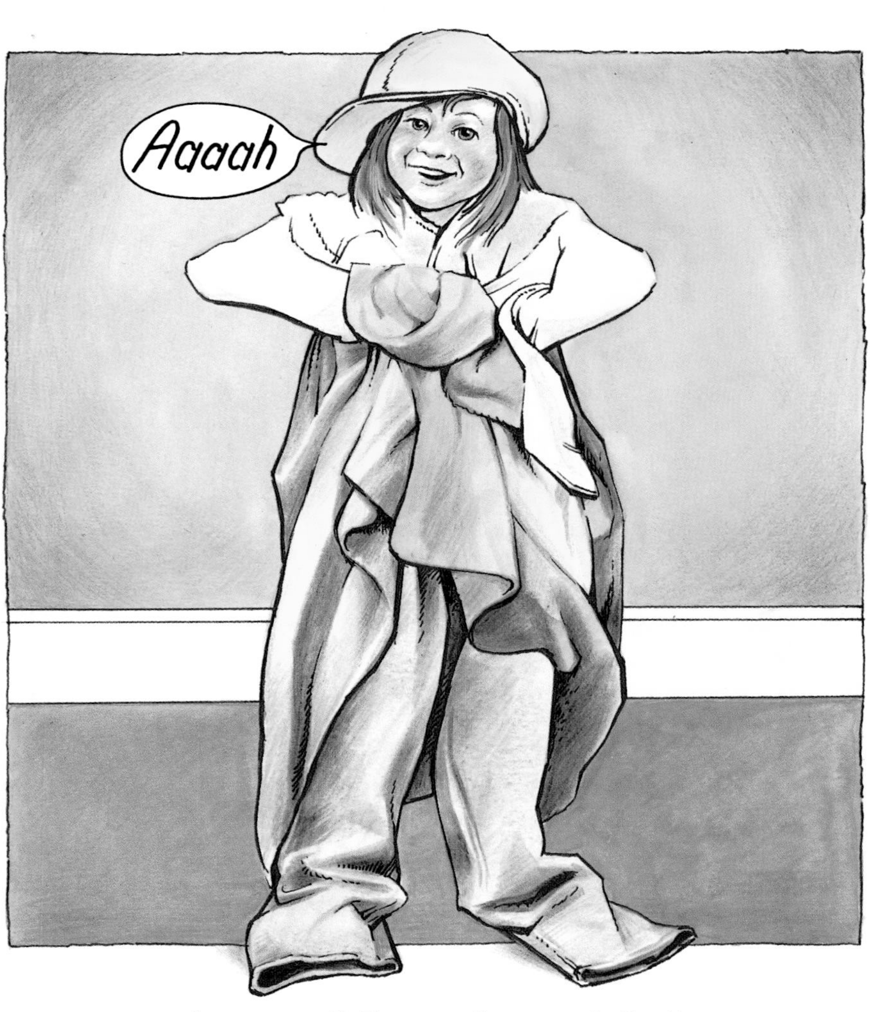

then Mom's skirt,

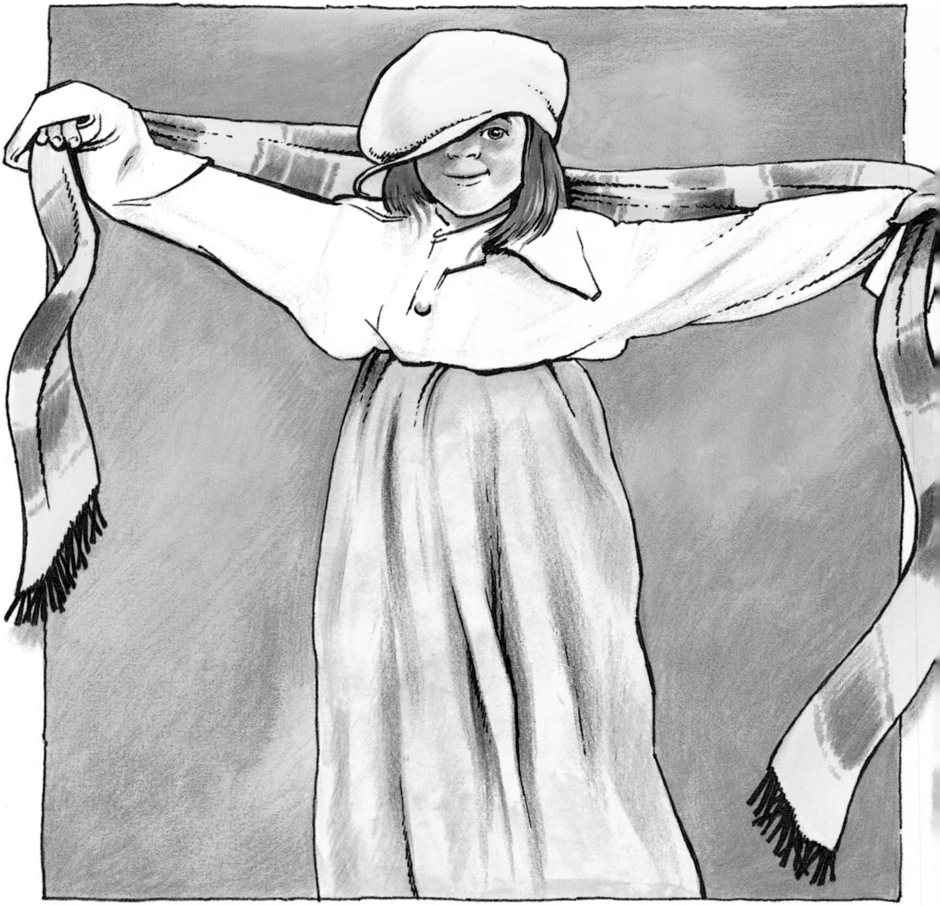

then Dad's scarf,

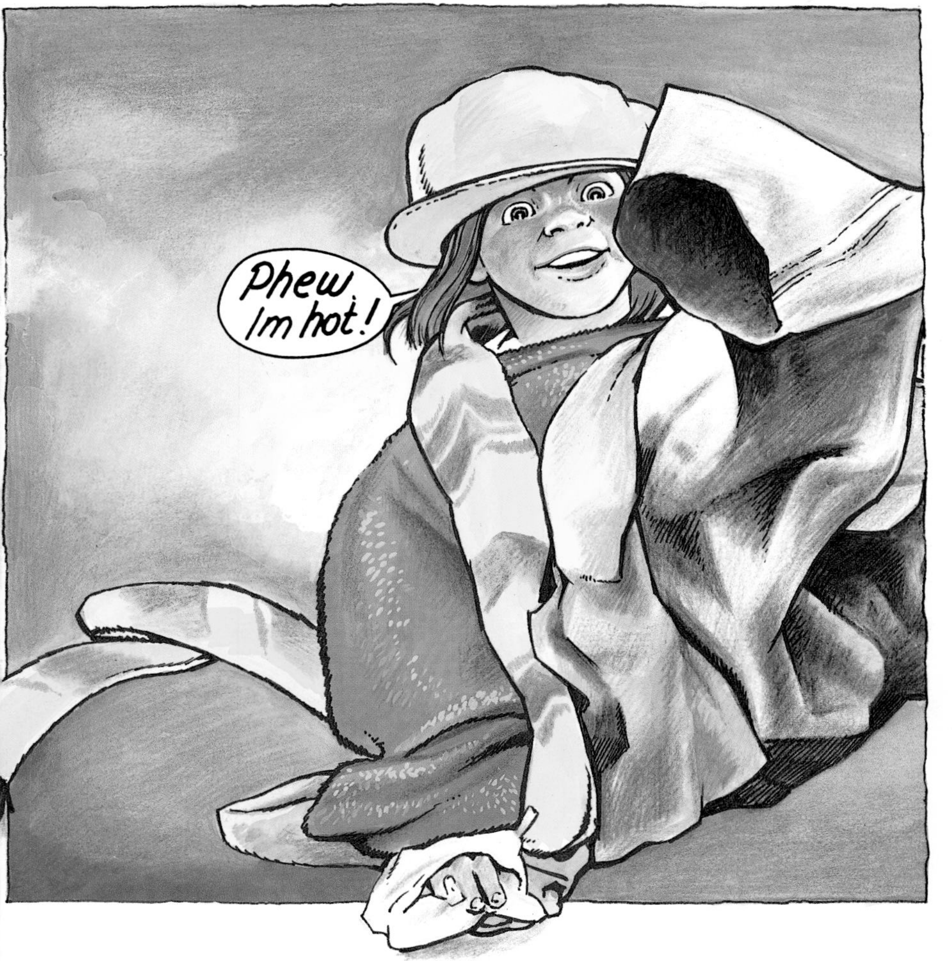

then Mom's sweater.
Too many clothes!

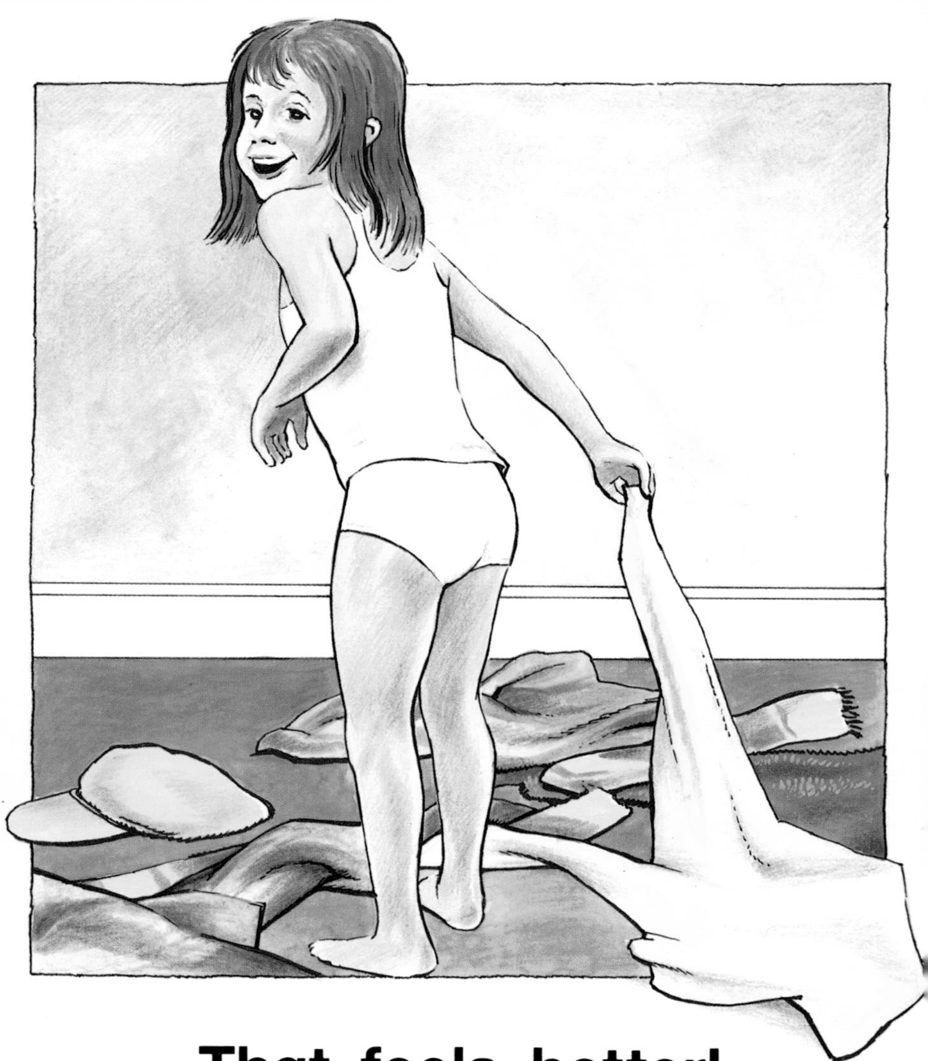

That feels better!